Fifty Shakes of Matrimony

Seine Emerald

FIFTY SHAKES OF MATRIMONY

Disclaimer

This publication is intended to provide helpful and informative material. It is not intended to diagnose, treat, cure, or prevent any health problem or condition, nor is intended to replace the advice of a physician. No action should be taken solely on the contents of this book. Always consult your physician or qualified health-care professional on any matters regarding your health and before adopting any suggestions in this book or drawing inferences from it.

The author and publisher specifically disclaim all responsibility for any liability, loss or risk, personal or otherwise, which is incurred as a consequence, directly or indirectly, from the use or application of any contents of this book.

Any and all product names referenced within this book are the trademarks of their respective owners. None of these owners have sponsored, authorized, endorsed, or approved this book.

Always read all information provided by the manufacturers' product labels before using their products. The author and publisher are not responsible for claims made by manufacturers.

Fifty Shakes of Matrimony

Seine Emerald

CONTENTS

CHAPTER 1: CAUGHT CHEATING, RECOVERING FROM HIM

"Did you think about him when we had sex?" my husband asks me.

It doesn't dawn on me at that point that it's the same question my ex-husband had asked me about Trevor way back in 1994, when I met the man who would become my husband after I divorced the first one.

I am standing near the front of my closet in our bedroom, backing into it in fact, farther away from his hurt-filled query and peering countenance. Trevor is sitting on our bed, right on the edge, looking up wearily for my response.

Shaking my head from side to side as I busy myself with ripping off my jeans, I don't yet let any words leak from my mouth. It would sound nice to deny his question – to look like the good and perfect Christian wife that so many women at my church pretend to be – but I cannot do it. I must break out of the pack of pretenders.

Plus, I know God is watching me, and I fear lying before Him more than lying to my husband.

"Don't ask me that," I say, continuing to shake my head.

"That means you did," Trevor says, looking down sadly. "How could you, Seine?"

For a split second I let the guilt wash over me. Here I am again, swimming around in the aftermath of another emotional affair, feeling like I'm taking all the guilt for getting too close to another Christian man who has played around in the absence of Trevor, who still doesn't attend church with me after all these years.

Why must I take pressure from people for admitting how I feel while they lay low with their sneaky secrets?

Wait a minute!

Why am I getting dressed-down by this wannabe Boy Scout who had admitted to going to one bachelor's party that had a naked woman right there in front of the guys, and going to a strip club when he was in New Orleans, all after we were married?

I'm not taking this crap lying down. Especially since Desmond and I never even got to the "good part" – thank God – and there was never any kissing or sex between us. Why do I feel like I take more heat than folks who actually went out and slept with someone other than their spouse? Perhaps that's just my paranoia. After all, I can feel how much the Lord is holding this marriage together right now.

"Don't sit there and pretend like you're a Boy Scout and that you've never had a bad thought!" I lob back at Trevor.

That gets him. He acquiesces.

"I know," he says.

After all, it was out of his own mouth that I felt like I pulled teeth the last time we got into it over a guy. That was when I confessed to falling for Kenny at work in 2004, back when I rejoined the company for an 8-month period.

In the wake of that confession, Trevor and I ended up having some good talks, and during one of them he finally admitted to imagining what a woman or two might look like without any clothes on.

Wouldn't it be sexier to think of them in a bikini?

That was my odd random reasoning upon listening to my husband's thoughts, but then again, I'm not a man – so I don't think like one. But that was back in 2004, and we've been through a lot since that point in our marriage and lives.

We had only been married eight years back then, coasting along, before anything too serious rocked our marital fellowship. That is, anything other than the wedge

I felt had been driven between us when I decided to seriously turn my life over to Christ in 2000 and join a large church – and Trevor decided not to attend with me most weeks.

When Kenny and I re-clicked at work, talking about all sorts of Christian situations – even trying to get an Indian developer saved by giving him "The Purpose Drive Life" and another believer's book for free, it was a good feeling.

Our "friendship" started getting a little uncomfortably close, however, and in the end, I was grateful when that contract assignment ended.

Today, on this day in November of 2011, I'm once again in the aftermath of an emotional connection that's been broken suddenly, away from a man that I never should have been that close to in the first place.

§ § § § § §

Desmond was in my life for 14 months, ever since the day I was first introduced to him as the leader of our technology team at church. He was only 29 then, a good 12 years younger than my 41 years – but with his ability to hang around and relate to older people, coupled with my blessed great genes of looking younger, we collided on a chemical level.

Yeah, it's true that a younger woman – other than his jealous wife – was in the running for his attention (along with any other cute women at church that caught his eye), but once my main competition moved away, the interests that Desmond and I shared in entrepreneurial things and Internet ventures grew off the chain.

Once again, I found myself spending my wedding anniversary away from my husband. Heck, I figured since Trevor and I hadn't planned anything special to celebrate anyway – nor had we arranged for a babysitter – it was simply easier to let the winds of opposition draw us apart, and me into the presence of another man.

It seemed innocent enough, and it was at first. The night that Trevor and I had been married 13 years, I was invited to a meeting held in the pastor's office, with about 10 key people in attendance.

"Oh, Seine's here," our pastor noted as I walked into the space.

I hesitated. "Is it okay?"

"Yeah, yeah, come on in," he said.

I took a seat in the corner at the oddly shaped table with four strange little uncomfortable black chairs that fit beneath each side like a puzzle piece. There I was, falling back, feeling the effects of being drawn into the inner sanctum of so-called important people at church.

The fading light shone through the spacious windows on my left, lighting up Desmond in his wearied but still energetic after-work state.

He fought for me that night, said I was instrumental in bonding two church locations together – and when the pastor tried to ask me about taking a job in the office, Desmond stood right there among everyone and spoke about how much he needed me to remain his administrative assistant instead.

The talk got so heated and was so oddly open, I put my hands to my mouth in a gleeful, bashful, embarrassed shame. A deacon offered Desmond a Kleenex from a rectangular box of tissue thrust in front of his face, saying that he was sweating.

No one perhaps knew how close Desmond and I had grown at that point, more than a year after we'd met. Maybe we didn't even know it ourselves, though the calls from him had become more frequent – and I smiled to myself when I'd check my cell phone and see a message that began with "Good morning, Seine!" from him.

I especially loved it when the text message was several hours old, coming in around 9:30 a.m. or so, showing that I was one of the first things on his mind. I liked it when I wasn't so desperate as to have already checked my texts too early in the morning, but had the wherewithal and had practiced enough self-control to not see the message for hours.

Inevitably, I'd be texting him right back, or better yet, hearing his sultry and joyful and playful voice in my left ear as he sat in his car at lunchtime or walked through the hallway at work on the way out to the parking lot, causing an echoing sound that sometimes forced me to ask him, "Where are you?"

It got so deep that when Desmond finagled to bring

me to the new church location where he worked – and I schemed to stay there another month – we got even more comfortable spending those dark days in the control room, many times just the two of us, talking about any number of things.

Sure, there were the chats about Christian books like "His Needs, Her Needs," and lots of good Scripture banter – but it all seemed to serve as a precursor to what we both knew was on the way. Or would've been on the way, if God hadn't have stopped it with a quickness.

The way we giggled over inane compliments or double-entendres reminded me of the same thing Trevor and I used to do when we met at our jobs in Chicago back in 1994 and the attraction was super-heated. When Trevor showed me how to open a paperclip and stick one end of the wire into a shallow well of black ink ensconced within a cartridge for the printer, we chuckled like adolescents.

It amazed me that I was feeling those feelings again with Desmond – a man who I just couldn't picture as my husband, no matter how attracted we became to each other. First of all, it wasn't just the age difference, but also the difference in height. I would look even taller than comedian Kevin Hart's girlfriend looming over him, leaning over and sliding my legs to the side to try and make up for what he lacked in height.

Nevertheless, when Desmond asked me if I'd seen "There's Something About Mary" and brought up the masturbation scene, it felt completely normal to have that conversation. We were growing closer on a more personal level, not like those staid and stuffy relationships with some church people who pretend they've never even uttered a curse word.

Somehow Desmond was likening the Ben Stiller's movie plight to my relationship with my husband, when the character was advised to please himself – (something I don't recommend, by the way) – before he went on a date so that he wouldn't appear desperate.

"You need that," Desmond kept stressing. "You need that connection with your husband."

"Don't come in here thirsty," I said, throwing out a word that I noticed younger people said. I was always trying to do that in his presence, to show him that I could relate – and not only pull slang from the 1970s, but from the twenty-tens as well.

He laughed along with me, and said, "Right!"

But what was he getting at? Had his wife tried to convince him at that point that I was after him or something? Heck, she only knew half the story. I know now that he was the type who didn't tell the whole truth, so help him God – yet I didn't know it then.

In my heart of hearts, I think it was all a set-up. Perhaps it was my cue to start complaining about a lack of sex with my Trevor or something – and the inroads for Desmond to tell me how much I deserve to be connected.

I really don't know what was truth and wasn't.

"One get the man, one get the dance," Christian rapper Lecrae would later rhyme, talking about a married man who put his arm around his wife as they walked with their child in the park. When the woman he'd been sleeping with showed up, he didn't even look her in the eye – not once ounce of admission or acknowledgement.

Yes, I ended up getting that stern, side-faced no-look that said everything from Desmond in time, the height of hypocrisy from a man whom I'd roll around on my marital bed talking to on the phone, falling for his sweet talk of why his wife should understand him making room for another woman in his heart.

He told me I was the closest person to him on the team. At first I wanted Desmond to say I was the closest person at church to him, but we both knew that would've meant I was closer to him than his wife – and that wasn't true.

"I really do love you," I said that day, and I should've known I was in trouble, sitting on the floor of my bedroom, confessing that kind of thing when I shouldn't have.

I heard Desmond smiling on the other end, glad that he'd finally drawn me into some kind of secret trap – a net of broken hearts and empty promises and bad dreams that he'd been collecting since the day he saw evil appear right in his own front yard as a little boy.

Yes, I was getting a little bit of the dance – but thank Jesus I didn't get the man. I got a much better one.

§ § § § § §

The proverbial stuff started hitting the famous fan when Desmond and I grew closer and closer, leaving my best friend Sherrie in the dust. Healthy and super light-skinned, Sherrie has a penchant for baking up the best delectable cupcakes and wedding desserts and the most amazing caramel nut brownies that could rival any Starbucks version you've ever tasted.

It was me that tried to encourage her to step out from under the wings of her hubby and begin selling those goodies around town – even shipping a few packages all around the country – and start making a tidy little profit from her business.

I've known Sherrie plenty longer than I knew Desmond. I met her way back around 2005, and though our friendship took time to develop, eventually it became seriously tight – especially after we joined the New Light Church together.

Sherrie even became a member of the technology team, and as new folks came and went, she and Desmond and I became a fast trio of friends. It was safe to have the three of us lingering in the parking lot on Wednesday nights or Sunday afternoons – and even during those other days when ministry meetings took up our time.

She was kind of like the chaperone I dragged to lunch with the Italian guy Kenny and me at my old job on my last day of work. That way, we could spend time together as friends without it looking suspicious.

However, as the flesh wants what it wants, and tries to rise up to defeat us before God's Spirit saves us, Desmond and I soon enough left Sherrie in the dust of the old location and grew closer to each other in our own, more private space of the new location.

There were times that we'd talk, just the two of us, for hours during service and afterward in the parking lot. Once we joked about leaving a teenage ministry worker in my minivan, entertaining Desmond's young son, perhaps, and playing games on her phone while we talked for an hour and twenty minutes.

"I felt sorry for her, but..." Desmond told me afterward, and we once again dissolved into laughs. The heart wants what the heart wants – and I was enthralled that we could spend the time it takes to almost watch an entire movie, gushing in one another's face, loving and admiring each other's brains (and other body parts) and getting so lost in how fast time can move.

All right, back to the stuff hitting the fan. (Expect rabbit trails into Desmond-land here and there.)

Sherrie was already carrying anger and jealousy, is my personal opinion, over Desmond sweeping me away to another church location and us fawning over our new "love" for one another.

I tried to talk to her about it one day in her car, after I'd left the new location and went back to the old one, seeing as though their later service was later than the service I'd left.

"When I'm seeing faces like this in my dreams, I just need to back up," she told me, and I took it to mean that she wanted to back away from me.

There it was – Sherrie was having the types of prophetic warning dreams about evil afoot that she'd had before about Desmond and another woman. It was the way I'd wanted my name to be connected to his – but this plan wasn't turning out like I'd hoped.

I wanted the fun without the fires of affliction, but when you're talking adultery, even non-sexual but emotional cheating, "Ain't no 'sicha' thing," as my grandfather might say.

My relationship with Desmond was bringing out a side of Sherrie that I just didn't like, but I eventually would realize was for the best. This tempest had to be stirred up within her – it was all a part of the plan to keep me from ruining my life and myself.

It started coming to a head when I left Desmond after some crazy crash driving event at the new location and headed back to the old location to hang out with Sherrie. During the after service time, Desmond called and joked with me, telling me he was stranded – knowing my nerves were already a bit jangled from watching a teenager crash his car into a curb mere hours before as he taught her how to drive.

"I was just about to tell you to stay right there, that I'd come get you," I laughed into the phone, covering my eyes with my hand to avoid Sherrie's gaze.

"You turned into like this schoolgirl around him," she'd tell me during many quiet nights later, as we dissected the events next to the fireplace in my living room.

But that day, I was all about Desmond. I continued chatting on the phone as Sherrie and I walked out to our cars, and I opened the electronic sliding door of my minivan and sat low on the floor, talking to him.

"I'm going to go," Sherrie said, tired of waiting. I smiled and waved her away.

Soon thereafter, when I texted and called Sherrie both on her home phone and cell phone to find out if I could schedule her for a certain location on a certain day, I got no response.

When she found out that Desmond and his wife had come over my house for dinner to hang out with Trevor and me, she got even more upset.

"Do you think it's wise to work so closely with someone you're attracted to?" she asked me, after I forced a smile out of her while offering her a plate of red beans and rice with freshly sliced tomatoes atop one afternoon.

Part of me felt sorry that I even confessed my feelings for Desmond to her, especially since it seemed she was throwing them back in my face. But perhaps she was only being my accountability partner – one of those terms Christians love, along with words like "transparency" that should be in the Christianese dictionary – like I felt I was doing when I called her to the carpet on actions in her past, statements she believed were being thrown up in her face as well.

At least I admitted my jealousy when Desmond liked the younger woman at first; I thought Sherrie was hiding her true ugly emotions behind a bunch of holy-sounding words. But that's neither here nor there, I didn't exactly bite back at her queries like I did my husband when he was acting all holier-than-thou.

It really reached the apex when Sherrie and I ended up at the same location one Wednesday night, and right beforehand she'd finally found her phone and discovered how to call me back. I wasn't having it, so I barely spoke to her the whole night.

The melee got back to Desmond – and by the following Wednesday night, he pressed me for details about what was going on.

"I feel something in my spirit," he said, sitting there in the darkness next to me. "I can sense it."

I hemmed and hawed around, avoiding his questions, thinking of what to say. I may have been head over heels and "wide open" for the man, but I was still smart enough not to say, "Sherrie's mad because you and I have been so close and I told her I was crushing on you."

Talk about a recipe for disaster. This was a man whose thigh I'd touched, and he'd tapped the side of my leg several times, leaving me hoping my muscles felt strong and taut.

We were alone, in the dark – and not strong enough to avoid the mutual attraction between us. I literally grew hot as I tried to explain the situation in safe terms to him.

"You see, you're like Jesus," I told Desmond. "And I'm like John. I'm the disciple whom Jesus loved. And Sherrie is like Peter. You know how they went at it sometimes."

Desmond tried to take in my biblical scenario, growing more confused. I decided on more direct, simpler terms, holding up my fingers to illustrate.

"At first there were five of us on the team, then four, then three," I described, with three digits in the air, folding one finger down until only two remained aloft. "Then you and I came down here…and it's just us two."

"Oh," he exclaimed. "You mean she's feeling like the odd-man out?"

"Yes," I said, glad that I'd given him an answer that satisfied his cravings, yet didn't tell too much of the danger afoot. I was happy he was no longer mad at me for holding out on him like he'd seemed minutes earlier, drinking his water slowly, pausing when I asked if he were mad at me.

"No," he'd said, after several seconds.

"That was a long 'no,'" I'd said, and the anger turned to laughter.

When Desmond darted out of the room and called the pastor, summoning him to talk to Sherrie at the other location, I had no idea he'd planned to do that. When he grabbed my arm and dragged me away from the soundboard in front of everybody as he chatted on the phone, I wondered if my arm inadvertently hit his belt or something else. I didn't want to know.

All I knew was that as he carted me down the hall arm-in-arm, it was too much. We were crossing all kinds of lines for two people that were married, but not to each other.

The mess with Sherrie would explode into a bunch of feelings the next morning, as she warned me against confessing my feelings to our leader. I couldn't take the lies and covering up any more, so during a conference call between the three of us, I confessed to Desmond – with Sherrie listening – that this trouble was because I felt an attraction to him.

Desmond didn't admit it then, but waited to call me later to say that he told our pastor that the attraction was mutual, and that he and I would be sent to separate church locations. Like two lovers ripped apart, our conversations grew more intimate, and we still found ways to see each other at the new church location.

"It doesn't have to be weird between us when we see each other," he said, but something had to give.

"It's Mr. McDonald again!" my son would say, handing me my Droid phone when Desmond called back unexpectedly, right after I'd hung up with him.

I didn't want my kids seeing their mom act in inappropriate ways like I'd seen both my parents act whilst growing up a time or two or three. Maybe that's why I gave myself away, turning to my laptop to write out the somewhat lusty, fictionalized tale of Desmond and I, and posted the screenplay online in a contest.

Accompanying the movie script was a trailer video, wherein I spoke of coming close to cheating on my husband, with somebody else's husband. Though I didn't expect it, someone from church found the video and my writings, and snitched on me to the pastor, who promptly – along with Desmond – kicked me off the team and out of that church location.

At first I cursed the cyber spy in my head, thinking they had a lot of nerve trying to curry favor with the head guy by telling on me. But then I learned to bless God for that person – even if it was Desmond's wife, or whomever was Googling me – because they were used as a pawn to get me away from a dangerous situation, and to help save two families from being destroyed.

Though I didn't see it in the days following being kicked out of church and thrust away from the people there who claimed to be as close as my family – especially during the mornings when I was so sad I could only drive to a nature park and lay my head against the driver's side window and sob – but that event would have the hugest impact on not only driving me back to God, but driving my marriage back closer together.

And beyond those bountiful blessings, it would have

an amazing impact on finally granting me the Hollywood career I craved. But not without a lot of miraculous days and magnetic drama first...

CHAPTER 2: SWEET DEAL

God is great.

I'm sitting here freaking out. It's been almost two years since the day that I got kicked out of the ministry and that church location – and the poster in my son's room with the date November 5, 2013, is a great reminder for me of wonderful things on the way.

For that's the Tuesday that it will be two years exactly since the day that Desmond texted me on Saturday, November 5, 2011 – one day after our pastor asked me to "take a break" from the ministry. I'd told Desmond that I'd call him later that day – for I had to wait for Trevor to leave for his golf game, so I could speak to him in private.

Once I did call him back, I apologized profusely for my writing – so blinded was I by wanting our relationship to continue.

"I just have one question for you, Seine," he said,

adding his trademark inflection on certain words. "What was your purpose for making that video and writing that script?"

I hadn't had the luxury of the time that has elapsed to view it all from the perspective I now possess. Just like our pastor, Desmond focused on the fact that I would have the nerve to actually write about my experiences – even though they were fictionalized.

"It was too much truth," he'd told me that day, when I told him it was a work of fiction.

Obviously his game was busted – and so was mine.

"I give myself away…so you can use me."

But instead of focusing on getting to the truth, Desmond and his pastor buddy devised schemes to try and make me disappear. That was the day Desmond said they needed space – "we" is what he called him and his wife, though prior to that there wasn't that much "we" in our conversations, especially not when he told me "*I* love you" or "*I* missed you" and so on.

I knew Desmond meant for me to stay away from the church location – like he was claiming the space for himself and his wife, since he was the team leader and I was just some kind of "peon" at the moment.

We'd seen each other the previous night at a ministry party, and I took special pains to avoid him. Desmond made a big show of having about five guys surround him like bodyguards as he walked right past me, his face facing straight ahead, a stern and determined look on his grill.

"What does he think I'm going to do to him?" I thought to myself.

Many days later, I realized that instead of assuming he was using those deacons – heaven knows what lies he'd told them – to protect his own little muscular self from any actions I'd take, perhaps he was using them to protect me from any angry actions he'd want to take against me.

It was all a crazy, silly ruse – and during that dark time, I knew I didn't have a leg to stand on, so I fell back. I tripped out over the few people acting all weirdly towards me – the selfsame ones who'd gladly taken gas gift cards from me, or had gotten rides in my minivan to or from church, and those who'd felt free to accept free popcorn and deep-dish pizza from me that I sent them from Chicago.

I knew in due time, God would turn it all around for the better – and He surely has thus far, even though the "fullness of time," my seeming 2-year punishment, isn't even over yet.

Sherrie thought I should've stayed at the church location and fought, but I was able to accept my part in the wrongdoing. I knew I let myself get too close to an attractive married man, and though I befriended his wife, I spent a lot more time with him. I felt renewed when the younger, handsome man paid me attention, and I lost sight of what I knew was right in God's eyes.

I had no basis to remain in that location, so I traveled

down about half-an-hour to the central base megachurch outside of Greenville, and quietly sat in the back pews as penance. During those first sermons after getting booted from the sanctuary I once loved, I could barely hold my head up. I was so broken and ashamed for the way I'd acted.

It was a nice night on Christmas Eve of 2011, when Trevor agreed to come to a late Saturday service at church, and we brought the kids, and I kind of felt like a normal family. I introduced him to a couple that had known me from the previous church location, and I was happy to have my husband by my side, seeing as though I'd been through so much drama – and felt like such a single woman or single mom all the times I had to go to church without my man.

In that time that I was ousted from church and felt so lonely, I began to do Bible studies alone in my minivan – just God and me, and grew from a weeping, sobbing mess to a woman looking like she wouldn't actually take a handful of pills and kill herself.

As I thought of the hubris of Desmond lying and spreading rumors that I was "evil" and the type of woman who "goes after married men" and such – all the while failing to mention the sexy things he'd said to me, like when he complimented my "subtle curves" – I knew the Lord would turn things around in a powerful way, without me needing to do a thing, besides cling to Him and his Word every day, like I'd been doing.

§ § § § § §

Isn't it funny how big changes seem to come on ordinary days?

It was a regular day in 2012 when I was cruising down my Facebook news feed, showing the variety of updates from friends and business associates and popular websites, when I saw one post that drew my interest. A friend had posted a photo of herself and a few other women, titling it the "McDonald's Going Away Party."

Could it be? I wondered. Could he actually be leaving town with his family, like I thought would happen, when the sudden thought of Desmond moving away came to me like a flash whilst pulling weeds in my garden.

Back then the thought of him leaving almost made me want to cry, and I'd discussed the sense I'd had that they would move away. He didn't make much mention of any such plans, but wavered between at first saying Greenville was the place he needed to remain for God to bless him – and thoughts of layoffs occurring at his job.

I'd prayed for his job and his family and his life and his sustenance many times. Sometimes it seemed I almost prayed for Desmond more than my own husband – but then I remembered to couple the prayers together and beseech God for the welfare and blessings for both of them.

By the time I saw that photo of Desmond and his "fam" going away, however, part of me was really pleased. I knew it meant that our already fractured relationship would finally be over, that he would just represent some sort of zany guy who blew into Peyton

Place for a season and tried to wreak havoc, but I was part of the main character crew remaining in Greenville, our town.

I'd already given up any online ties I had to him, starting with the time Desmond and his wife blocked me on Facebook. I desperately looked at my statistics tracker in the days and weeks after I was dumped from being Desmond's #1 technology team chick – and I felt so good when I'd see stats showing that someone with a MacBook in his area had been on my blog. In my silly mind at the time, I viewed our blogs as our sole means of communication, seeing as though I'd "blown up our spot" and we could no longer see each other, nor text, necessarily.

I'd write various blog posts with crazy pictures, displaying my pensive and mournful state. I didn't know whether it was Desmond or his wife checking out my writing – sometimes it seemed as if both were – but it made me upset when I'd see that he hadn't checked it for days on end.

So much for the guy who'd cried on the other end of the phone with me, telling me he felt "devastated" and that it felt like his "heart dropped to his stomach" when he saw my video.

"I still care..." he trailed off into tears, but later said, "Hold on," as if to check that his wife wasn't eavesdropping.

Yes, it was a lot of dancing indeed. I knew all the checking up wasn't healthy for me, especially when I saw a Psalm 75:7 Scripture on one of his blog's posts that was still set up to be emailed to me:

But God is the judge: he puts down one, and sets up another.

Wait – what?

Was Desmond actually gloating over me being kicked out of the ministry and hinting at his own deacon-training track by using that Word of God against me?

I couldn't believe it. Not only was he not apologizing for the major part he played in our emotional adultery, he was going around telling Sherrie (and God knows who else) that God has a way of exposing people, and that my spirit was wrong, and that now that the "evil" had been excised from the congregation, things would get better.

They only got worse at that location after I was booted out.

My life was improving, however, only by the grace of God. When I woke up the morning of December 25, 2011, I saw the rendition of Akiane's Jesus on my wall, and it was like I could feel Christ telling me not to do any more cyber sleuthing on Desmond – so I didn't, and it was freeing.

I stopped checking my stats to see where visitors were coming from, and I made sure to unsubscribe from his blog, and to delete that LinkedIn request to connect that he'd sent me eons ago.

The Lord was telling me that it wasn't making me feel

any better by checking each day to see if Desmond had most likely read what I wrote – or blogging about things in hopes that he would read it, or pick up the subtle hints I'd included that showed that I had read what he'd written on his business' Facebook page. It had been 26 days since the December day that he'd texted me out of the blue whilst Trevor was in Miami, and it took me a little while to even read the multiple texts.

Desmond thanked me for the "GOOD" work I'd done in the ministry, and for all that I'd taught him. I did the same, praying for his family and stuff.

"I receive that!" he wrote back in his traditional overexcited way, and I left it at that. I just let it be, not texting him back again.

And it's good enough, because soon enough, although he still broke down and asked Sherrie "How's Seine?" on New Year's Day, he was already trying to get his hooks into another woman on the ministry team, spending time on FaceTime with her and everything, under the guise of helping her "clone herself" in business, and other lines that he gave me and others.

Good riddance, said I, leaning on the words to "bless those who curse you and pray for those who spitefully use you" by the time of his departure. Of course I wondered if Desmond had gotten laid off from his job, and if that's what drove him and his family away from here and back home to Boston.

"They were removed," Sherrie said, repeating the words she believed God told her about the couple.

These days, I'm grateful for the lesson he brought to my life: the fact that I never ever want to be involved in anything close to that again. I want to succeed in keeping a platonic, friendly relationship with anyone I work with or go to church with, and I never want to cause a wife pain, no matter what kind of Casanova Lothario she's married to.

I'm so glad they are gone – and a short time later, I would be overjoyed about another couple's departure as well.

§ § § § § §

"Did you hear about Pastor Jameson?"

That's what one friend who was briefly on and off the technology team asked me one hot July 2012 day when I saw her in Wal-Mart. You could've called it a tech team reunion, because we stood with another member of the tech team who'd gotten kicked off the team early for living in sin with the father of her children.

I'd actually kind of looked down on her, or rather, felt smug in my married and supposedly not-sinning state. Little did I know that I should've been studying that Scripture that says, "Be careful when you stand lest you fall" back then.

Either way, that sultry summer day, I was glad I didn't skip walking over to the ladies and getting in on the gossip, like I initially considered doing. But these two chicks were cool, not like any judging women who treated me like their stuff didn't stink.

"No, what?" I asked. "I didn't go to church Sunday because I was in Chicago."

"He's trying to get all the people to go with him and start his own church," she answered.

What she was telling me was so foreign to my ears that I could barely take it in. I resorted to a surprising line in the popular YouTube video called "David After Dentist."

"Is this real life?" I asked.

"Yep," she answered, not finding my query strange.

There it was, the same pastor who had railed at me for creating that writing revealing my true relationship with "his boy," the pastor who didn't show complete compassion when I asked for an end-date to my prison sentence of being kicked off the team.

"For how long?" I'd asked him.

"Until!" he almost yelled back, as if to say, "Your punishment will last as long as I say it will last."

Back then, I took my penance in hand, and wondered if he didn't think something would happen one day whereby he might have to walk in church with his wife and not be the "top dog" on top of the world – but that life could actually knock him down a peg or two or twenty.

That day about a year ago, it seems some of the knocking down had occurred. I find turnabout being fair play, seeing as though Pastor Jameson's church has moved around a few times, and he's not the "big man on campus" connected to the bigger man on campus anymore.

But I don't want hate in my heart. If there's one thing I've learned, is that there are two sides to every story, so I don't take any one person's version of anything – especially if they are trying to disparage one sole being in order to hide their own sins.

In the wake of all this church drama, I've felt comfortably ensconced in the home I share with my husband and our kids. If getting out of the house back in 2010 in order to help start that new church location was exciting and thrilling, the dark day of 2011 that exposed my emotional affair showed me that there's no place like home.

At first it felt weird to stay home on Wednesday nights and not jet over to the church location to help set up, chat with folks and listen to the pastor preach a sermon. But within a few weeks, it felt supremely comfortable to stay home Wednesday nights and catch an episode of *Modern Family* with Trevor, laughing and tossing back a glass of wine if I wanted.

Same thing on Saturday nights. I no longer needed to worry about trying to get to bed early so that I could get up and out of the house by 7 a.m. so I wouldn't get a dressing down by Desmond, when he felt like he needed to stretch his leadership muscles. I liked hanging out with the crew, but some of the rules and attitude coming down from the top was for the birds.

Trevor and I got closer once again, getting into the habit of watching SNL and having a drink, or staying up late going on date nights – one of those things that came out of our marriage counseling sessions. We ended up only going a handful of times, but hopefully that was enough to help get us back on a better track that where we were before the infraction.

§ § § § § §

Of course I had to write about it. God had transformed my mornings in the car with Him into a time where I'd drive to various trailheads around this gorgeous Greenville area and study some Scripture, write out my thanks for all the things He's done, plus any dreams I'd had the night before that felt noteworthy.

Then I'd take off walking or biking down a trail – something I learned to do during the rain, sun or snow most days. I'd pray in tongues sometimes, or other times think up storylines. That's how "Church People" was born, a series of books that chronicled what I'd been through with Desmond – fake names and mistakes and all.

The first book was selling pretty darn well and steadily in Amazon's Kindle store after I published it, more than 100 copies per month before its popularity shot through the roof after one simple mention by Tyler Perry, in an off-handed manner in a YouTube video interview that turned everything around for me, just in perfect timing.

By the time I was contacted by the big wig's acquisition rep via the email address I'd hopefully placed in the Kindle book's description, I didn't have to wonder whether it was fake or some kind of phishing scam – I knew it was real, especially once I researched her name and we talked via phone.

I knew the book about church people that I was writing during February 2013 was different and had a special amount of favor that existed within the words. That's because I wrote it directly after walking in the woods with God.

I would imagine Jesus right there with me walking in front of me, like I did on the occasions when I used to ride my bike in the woods on a biking and walking trail down a nature path, when I would imagine Christ floating around me in a brilliant white robe, resplendent and powerful, pulling my bike forward.

"Help me, Jesus," I would pray, practicing the presence of Jesus the way I learned to do in Pastor Joseph Prince's "Unmerited Favor" book.

This time I *actually did it*, not just *talked* about it, like I did during the days when I spoke of Jesus being right there with Desmond and me, and then promptly forgot our Savior could see all of our flirting around.

During those days in the woods, the Lord gave me strength and energy as he does every day and I was able to take that power directly from the woods and bring it home and write out exactly the next plot twists, containing my deepest thoughts and feelings.

Whether they were right or wrong didn't necessarily matter, it seemed what mattered was getting them out of me and onto the page then onto that Word document and uploaded to that Kindle Direct Publishing module for the world to see, buy, read and relate to on an intimate level, as they nodded their heads "Yes!" and related to some of the same events I'd experienced in life.

So the books sold more than 100 copies per month at first – and then as soon as that simple mention came to life, when Tyler Perry sat in his gorgeous California home overlooking the ocean, chatting with Oprah about something mundane, he let the name of my book drip eloquently from his pretty "Madea" shaped lips. He spoke of being obsessed with it and not getting enough. I watched my stats go through the roof after that, and never ease up.

Once Tyler Perry and Oprah showed interest in the book, it took off through the stratosphere. The sales hit 10,000 to 100,000 per month.

And that was only the beginning. Not only did Oprah buy rights to the story for a feature film produced by Harpo Films, but she also collaborated with Tyler Perry and Bishop TD Jakes and the "Produced by Faith" author who is married to Meagan Good – DeVon Franklin, a pastor, and a renaissance man who holds a high position within Sony Pictures.

They all collaborated to create a potent one-hour OWN TV drama series based around the book, which lends itself perfectly to a Shonda Rhimes *Scandal* type of drama that is set inside a mega-church. Mega-power of God coupled with mega-Christianity and mega-drama, all rolled into a smart and complex yet infinitely watchable TV show unlike anything ever seen.

People will experience the hand of God even through their TV screens, or more likely, iPhone screens, iPad screens and MacBook screens as they watch the show – one made by Christians who are unafraid to include biblical references like speaking in tongues and powerful baptisms in the Holy Ghost, interspersed with episodes about the kind of "Holy Roller hypocrites" that we all know exist, claiming the Kingdom of God.

It's the perfect time and the atmosphere is primed and ready for such a long-running, Emmy-nominated, record-breaking viewership of a show.

As it is written, "I have made you the father of many nations." Abraham acted in faith when he stood in the presence of God, who gives life to the dead and calls into existence things that don't yet exist.

My mega-book-and-TV-series-and-feature-film-deal couldn't have come at a more perfect time. The advance monies of $100,000 for the multi-book deal alone not only took care of the money that I owed American Express and the nearly $6,000 minimum payments I was staring down on my green card and gold card, but it also paid for all taxes we owed and all of our credit card debts -- as well as bought us a new roof on our home and a sorely needed exterior and interior paint job to boot.

At that point I had been hiding what I owed American Express from Trevor, because I just wanted to take care of it myself and I felt like I just wanted it paid off and paid off ASAP. And wasn't it just like God to bring that huge blessing into my life even after I had done plenty of things wrong – but still He showed his unmerited grace and favor through the blood of Christ Jesus so strongly in my life.

As we readied our Greenville home for sale and hired contractors to fix it up nicely, we relocated to a nearby home with an in-ground pool off Joyman Lane overlooking a gorgeous valley of perfectly manicured golf course greens replete with deer and doe and fawns, along with bald eagles, robins, cardinals and blue heron frolicking around the winding Seneca River in full view of our walkout patio and master bedroom and my writing room.

So I breathed a big sigh of relief knowing all those bills were paid, and that I was tromping along on the path that I felt the Lord had already prepared me for, when He had previously encouraged me to begin running again to lose weight.

I wrote on the calendar every Friday my weight as it dipped from 174 pounds down to 169 pounds down to 164 pounds and 152 pounds and so on. By the time we readied ourselves to relocate to California, Trevor had joined me on our matching power folding treadmills, running and then weightlifting – causing both of us to drop excellent amounts of weight before we made our

Left Coast debut.

I remembered what Renée Zellweger said when she was asked how she gained 30 pounds for her pivotal role in *Bridget Jones's Diary,* and she simply stated that she stopped running. Well, starting to run again is what helped me to drop 40 pounds over several months, and my husband took it easy with his heart health, became inspired and began to love running again, too.

He also started lifting weights, even heavier amounts than I did, as we ate healthy and delicious foods and drank good supplements. Trevor began looking a lot hotter with his physique, like Will Smith, and I rivaled Halle Berry in the sensuality department.

So we fell into a total honeymoon phase – a miracle as we celebrated our 15th wedding anniversary by searching around the Los Angeles area for a gorgeous, God-filled home to rent, praying all the while that the pilot for the TV show would be picked up as a series and that the viewers would love it and that the ratings would fly through the roof.

§ § § § § §

Another beautiful thing about having several months in Greenville before we needed to relocate to California was that Trevor and I had time to ourselves to bond and relax. And also I was able to buy the kind of Indique "organic curl" weave hair that I loved.

I had it dyed the perfect shade of golden blond

highlights and dark brown color that matched my natural hair just as I liked it. It would be perfect for the California sun, and I was able to take my time integrating it in the way I like into my hair nice and thinly as my own hair began to thicken with the special formulas and formulations of Minoxidil and other creams that I purchased for my hair.

During that time of preparation, like Esther preparing to see the king, I made a visit to a very kindly plastic surgeon who performed the Benelli Breast Lift "donut mastopexy" concentric type of breast lift I always wanted, the kind that doesn't require implants or doesn't create too much scarring like that anchor type of nipple-moving surgery that I did not want.

It was such an easy outpatient service and it didn't hurt that much at all and the recovery time was very minimal. I was able to get back to doing some of the regular things I loved in no time, like running, swimming and working out.

§ § § § § §

Our lives are finally taking off in the direction we wanted them to take off. In no time, I'll be returning to California with my family – but this time into show business, working in Southern California with creative types of writers, working in the writers room where I always wanted to be, this one with a gorgeous view and full of like-minded cool people that are also believers in Christ.

And Holy Spirit filled, good-looking, great-looking people – not sinful, carnal Christians. And not a religious demon in the bunch, you know the type, preaching a long list of do's and don'ts while hiding their our horrible sins in the closet.

I'm looking fierce and fabulous and my husband is looking and feeling great as well. We are both healthy, and the move has injected such excitement and passion and love into our union, because we have something so great to look forward to once more.

California here we come.

Goodbye… Greenville!

I wonder what kind of people we'll meet there. And I wonder if we'll stay for good…

CHAPTER 3: I KNOW YOU WANT ME

Being a staff writer on a (all fingers crossed in the prayer position) successful one-house drama is the perfect job.

I don't have the pressure that celebrities face: There's no need to look absolutely perfect at all times, and no need to be anorexically thin for the cameras – and perhaps the best part of all, I can walk down the street and have my privacy with my family and friends, and still get paid nearly a comparable salary with some of the movie and TV stars who do have to put up with such fame.

Trevor is happily playing Mr. Mom at home, picking the kids up from the wonderful Christian school of performing arts we found that they both adore, and teaching them how to play golf and tennis in the off hours.

I, on the other hand, feel positively brand new and

alive being able to create stories and plot twists and dialogue surrounded by an enormous, dynamic, special group of supremely talented people.

When we get stuck or too hungry to create, we simply take a break and go grab delectable salads down the street, or even hold our meetings right on the beach in Malibu.

I'm experiencing the sensation of being able to not only breathe again, but also inhale and exhale deeply in a new way that I've been waiting for my entire 44 years on this planet, like when a person finally finds their long-lost family members.

I am swimming in an ocean with calming, bath-water temperature clear liquid – I am frolicking in the bubbly, salty shores with people who don't pause and furrow their brows when I use terms like "backstory" or "character arc" or "flashback" or "flash-forward" and such.

Instead, they expound upon my thoughts even further, with more depth, like synergized souls.

§ § § § § §

It's a beautiful thing that I'm able to throw myself into my job so much lately, because Lord knows I haven't thrown myself onto Trevor in a good long while. I don't like to count the days or weeks it's been since we've made love, but I hope and pray it hasn't been months.

I don't want to depress myself, and although I know

there are times that I could grab him fresh out of the shower (or give him a sponge bath) and bring him back to myself, at times I think of that interesting verse from the lonely wife featured in Song of Solomon 8:4, who advised:

Daughters of Jerusalem, I charge you: Do not arouse or awaken love until it so desires.

There's something about that Bible verse that reminds me of not going after my husband sexually – if I'm reading it correctly – but to do all I can to make myself as attractive and becoming to him as possible, and pray and act to set the atmosphere to make him want to approach me.

When my husband and I haven't "connected" in a little while, it makes me feel longingly toward him – or just wanting the desire of being wanted. Men are supposed to chase women – correction – men are supposed to chase their wives, not the other way around.

He who *finds* a wife *finds* a good thing – whoops, I interestingly wrote "God thing" at first, and that fits just fine. Anyway, Proverbs 18:22 makes it seem like the man should be looking and the wife should be found, not out chasing and proposing and looking desperate.

These days, when I kick off work early, or on weekends, when the kids are off doing fun stuff with their friends at camp, and Trevor and I steal away for a pitcher of margaritas at a nearby Mexican restaurant, I love it when that feeling surges once more.

"You're so pretty," Trevor told me one day, gazing

into my eyes, adopting his soft voice. "Such a pretty face," he repeated.

The male waiter who came close enough to us to overhear the sweet talk as he cleared away some dishes smiled in spite of himself.

"Pretty brown eyes," I told Trevor, as I often do when I admire his deep amber hued irises.

Before long, the candles were lit and water sloshed out of our new garden tub as the gray clouds moved slowly outside our windows above our heads.

Reconnected, and it feels so good.

§ § § § § §

Success!

Favor ain't fair, as they say.

"Church People" just experienced an unprecedented blessing: the ABC network order seven episodes of the series that will run concurrently with the series on OWN – especially seeing as though not everyone has access to Oprah's channel.

It sort of reminds me of when "The Bible" was featured on The History Channel and Lifetime TV.

This cast of characters in the writer's room is not what I expected. It's raining men. Paul, Apollos and Peter. I kid you not.

Apollos is my test, the one that I knew would always appear after my previous three failures and emotional crushes and affairs, ones that didn't involve sex or kissing but still probably weren't healthy in God's eyes.

And just like I expected this guy had it all over the other ones – not only does he have the looming height, lithe muscular build and the lighter skin that I tend to favor, but also quite the intelligent brain.

He's also got the wedding band to match, just like the new 3-carat emerald cut clean diamond that Trevor placed on my left hand during a candlelit ceremony celebrating our 15th wedding anniversary at the beach at dusk in a truly romantic and moving dinner for two.

I know this is a test, perhaps nowhere near as hard as the test that Jesus successfully accomplished when the devil tempted him in the desert, but a test nonetheless and one that he has fully equipped me with surpassing.

Now I get to practice all those tactics I've learned about in books, like imagining and practicing how I will spurn and rebuke any advances made towards me, instead of rehearsing love scenes in my head with any man other than my husband.

I will continue to keep my eyes open during sex and actually look at Trevor's gorgeously glossy and wavy black hair, supple and thick, and not let my mind trail off like I've done in the past.

§ § § § § §

I remember the words Trevor's ex-girlfriend told me she said to a married male coworker whom she was hinting that she never messed around with, as if trying to make up for some untold sin that she never revealed to Trevor.

"We should go out to dinner sometime," is what the married guy supposedly asked her, a woman I'll call Monica.

"Me and you and *your wife* should go to dinner sometime," Monica allegedly responded.

Who knows what really happened there – and writing about Trevor's ex makes me remember how cute and desperate she was to keep him. She had a tight little body, but not like mine – still, none of that superficial stuff mattered. You've seen one pair of boobs or one butt, and you've nearly seen them all.

In the end, Trevor and I had destiny on our sides. But it's neither him nor me that keeps our marital bed undefiled – it's God alone giving us the strength to do so when the enemy would try and make us think otherwise. I've nearly fallen for that routine in the past that has sent at least two couples we know off to divorce court – good friends that have children, ones we thought might have stood the test of time.

"You deserve somebody hotter than her," the evil one might whisper to a guy, trying to dissuade him from sticking with the woman who has borne his children and brought him hot meals to his bedside.

"You need some hot sex now," Beelzebub may say to a woman who feels unappreciated and unloved, lusting over some guy's eighteen-pack in the weight room.

Yet there's a quieter and still more powerful voice that whispers in Trevor's ear and my ear and your ear, dear reader, which speaks the voice of truth.

"I will not suffer thy foot to be moved," our great God reminds us. "I that keepeth thee will not slumber."

And so we wait, keeping smart and safe and holy and waiting for bad feelings of horniness and desire for wrongdoing to quell – praying all the while, knowing that this too shall pass. It always passes, at times sooner than we'd planned – and once again we've been giving the power to overcome.

§ § § § § §

I'm operating in the Mighty One's power right now in the writer's room, the gorgeous Valley View conference room overlooking the water – the one where we can see the sun dipping below the Pacific Ocean some days when we're closing out a pivotal script – or having a table read with the actors.

The subtext is thick, and we liberally borrow from feelings and relationships going on right in our writer's room to put them on screen.

I find it odd that this trio of men – Apollos, the married one, and the single Peter and Paul – seem pretty enamored with me, although we've got the big-boobed and wide-eye romantic Jessica on staff as well.

Octavia rounds out our crew of writers – a married, plump, no-nonsense kind of woman. She knows her stuff and has helped guide me through this process of being a successful Hollywood writer of a one-hour drama.

We all know our alter ego roles and on screen personas, except for other main characters that are also clearly stolen from real-life experiences. Take for instance the episode that helped "Church People" become a starring vehicle for Meagan Good, who starred as an actress that ended up with "the man," the pastor that plenty of other women in the sanctuary had their eyes on marrying.

Once it was announced that Meagan's character would marry the handsome and smart young rising star in the church, a bunch of women didn't show up the next Sunday, a similar storyline that former rapper Ma$e – Pastor Mason Betha – experienced upon announcing his engagement.

A portion of the women who remained in the megachurch featured in the fictional Los Angeles house of worship in the TV series began hating on the main character, talking about the sexy way she dressed and stuff.

"The evil church chicks are just mad they didn't get

him," I explain during our writing session.

"Agreed," Apollos says, smiling at me from ear to ear.

"I've got a storyline," Jessica chimes in. "Why don't we show Dana and Deacon Kevin slowly and gradually entering into an adulterous affair? Their characters are already ripe for the plucking...their noses wide open for each other."

Uncomfortable, edgy silence follows her comment. Everyone in the room knows we are a group of writers talking about scenarios of each other – we are a movie inside a movie.

The character of Dana is largely based upon me and my personality and experiences, while Deacon Kevin not-coincidentally shares many aspects of Apollos' mind, will and emotions.

"We see people cheating on their spouses every day – a romp in the rectory is just so *Scandal*," I say.

Loud laughter breaks the tension.

"You know what's even better and sexier? Unrequited, platonic love," I answer myself. "It's more fascinating to me to show how people hold out and don't cheat."

"That's it!" Octavia jumps in. "That tension will help the viewers and help the show last longer."

"Yep," says Peter, the older, unmarried "player-player" of the group. "Remember *Moonlighting*? It went downhill after Cybill Shepherd and Bruce Willis slept together."

He covers his mouth and smiles. "Their *characters*, I mean."

"That wasn't the reason for the *Moonlighting* curse," Jessica counters. "The problem was that after the main characters did sleep together, the story got stale."

"Well let's keep it fresh and sexy," Apollos says, looking directly at me.

"Wow, that's what I tell my husband Trevor all the time," I interject, flashing my ring for emphasis. "Let's keep it fresh and sexy."

A lobbed flirtation seemed to have been sent back with a big old "talk to the hand" type of kind rejection. I could get used to this, learning how to seriously be a good Christian wife by counting my blessings and not messing them up.

This is sweet.

The devil might be trying to dangle these tempting characters in my face, but God is showing me how to easily dissuade that mess. Heck, I finally understand the great things my Maker has provided me, and by his grace and favor and mercy alone, I'm not messing any of it up.

§ § § § § §

"I ordered in dinner and I lit the fireplace," Trevor

tells me via phone as his voice fills my 2013 Porsche Cayenne SUV with the panoramic sunroof.

"It's gotta be 100 degrees in Calabasas today!" I exclaim with laughter, a cute tickly feeling in my tummy.

"No, it wasn't that hot," he says. "It's cooling off. Plus, you know I like it hot."

"I know you do, baby," I continue, flirting with the man. "I'll be home soon."

When I arrive at our home and click my kitten heels across the stonework of the kitchen floor into the sunken living with deep, luxurious carpeting and out onto the patio, I see that not only does Trevor have the outdoor fireplace roaring, but he's also lit citronella candles and bamboo Tiki torches in strategic places in the backyard lawn, with a group of them shaped into a heart.

"Oh my goodness!" I exclaim, my silky halter dress blowing in the breeze of the Santa Ana winds. "What is all this, my lovely husband?"

We kiss full on the lips as Trevor motions with a strong arm and hugs me, then slides a patio chair with protected rubber bottoms out from the dinner table for me to sit on.

"It's all for you," he says. "I ordered your favorite food."

Upon first sight of the In-N-Out Burger trademarked half-wrapped burgers and fresh carton of French fries and drinks that display palm trees blowing in the wind, I crack up.

I throw my arms around his neck and kiss him over and over again. He hugs me closer, tightly around my waist, drawing me into his firm torso and grip.

Trevor isn't rushing me off or in a hurry to get to the next thing, like that scene in the movie *Vacation* that we joke about, when Chevy Chase's character is in a rush to get a funeral eulogy for Aunt Edna over with, so he starts babbling about, "Yea, and though the Hindus speak of Karma…"

When we naturally release one another, I sit and he sits across from me, pulling a bottle of champagne from a silver bucket of slightly melted ice.

"That's the same thing Beyoncé ate," I say. "She had In-N-Out Burger with champagne."

"We're in good company, heh?"

Trevor pops open the bottle and fills two flutes with the sparking, gold bubbly liquid. We hold them aloft and click.

"To us, together," he says.

"Amen!" I confirm.

We both offer a little giggle as we chitchat about our days, about our kids, and all the latest sayings and tidbits that I'd normally be offering to Trevor in this situation after a long hard day at work.

It's then that I recognize the look in his eyes: There's a new appreciation within his stare as he honestly pays attention to my face when we speak, and doesn't fiddle around distractedly with his Samsung Galaxy phone, or just glance at any nearby sports scores or ESPN replays.

I understand that our roles have somewhat reversed – finally. No longer am I the sort of desperate and needy work-from-home wife and mom looking forward to her husband coming home for a dose of further entertainment.

The years of me waiting longingly for Trevor to come home when our children were babies have long past. And praise God that the days of him hanging out after work and stopping at the bar with colleagues without even giving me the courtesy of a phone call are long gone. We went through enough arguments over that behavior in 2008, even though Trevor claims he didn't go out that often, it felt often enough for a woman home with kids for the better part of the day.

No, Trevor's heart health issues were one of the things Jehovah Rapha, the Lord our Healer, used to help turn him around from that hurtful behavior. I'm so glad I stuck through it all; I really love the man.

And look where we are today: With me feeling like I'm harvesting the fruits of my homemaker and full-time mom labors, seeing as though I'm the one out and about making money and working with fascinating people and having new, wonderful experiences left and right.

Trevor's been able to get what he says he's wanted for years: a break from the rat race, time to simply golf and relax and be with the kids and figure out what he'd really like to do in life. Meanwhile, I'm so grateful to God for allowing me to bring in a bunch of money – more than ever before – to our household income.

Life is sweet.

"Take your pick," Trevor says, fanning out a bunch of brochures on the table, surprising me out of my quiet reverie.

"What are these?" I ask, picking up a brochure to see a picturesque photo of a Sonoma Valley spa, a stucco building with vines creeping up the side.

Another brochure contains a delightful photo of an outdoor whirlpool beneath a covered circular gazebo. Still a different brochure displays a photo of a woman lying face down on a massage table with black stones aligned along her spine.

"Don't you remember when we stayed in the wine country all those years ago?" he asks me.

"Oh yeah, Napa Valley was beautiful," I said. "And then remember the Villagio Inn and Spa, when we sat out on the patio and smoked a cigar and drank white wine and talked? I'll always remember that time with you…"

"I loved their fluffy beds," Trevor reminisced.

"And the fireplace!" I recalled. "And those tall, strong

women that massaged us in the spa."

We both crack up at the memory.

"Well, you choose the spa in Sonoma or Napa, and we can stay there a whole week," he says. "It's all set."

"What's all set?"

"Mommy and Daddy already agreed to fly out to watch Sean and Kayla, so we can just pack and fly on up," he says. "Or, we can drive up the coast if you'd prefer."

I set the brochures back on the table and take another sip of bubbly.

"I can't go now, we're at a pivotal point in the season," I say.

"Heck, you're the series creator!" Trevor says emphatically. "You should be able to leave whenever you want."

"But honey, we're trying to turn these initial seven episodes they've ordered into 100 episodes – we want a long, successful run," I explain.

Trevor sets his glass down on the mosaic table carefully.

"I know, I understand," he softens his tone. "It's just you've been working so hard lately. Can't they get along without you for a week or two so you can get away?"

"Well, yeah, sure," I hesitate. "But I love what I do – I don't want to miss anything."

"So when exactly do you plan on slowing down and spending some family time?" he queries.

I pick up a French fry and bite the tip.

"Why do I have to slow down?" I ask. "I feel like I already did that for nearly 12 years when the kids were younger."

"And I liked that," he admits. "I liked having you home, having you there when I got home. I want that again."

"What? What are you saying?"

"I mean, you've already got the book deals to fulfill, the movie will be coming out," he explains. "I think you should let the staff writers handle all the remaining episodes."

Shock washes over my body like an electric wave. I take a big gulp of my drink.

Trevor wants me to quit my job.

"I can't quit my job!" I nearly shout.

"Seine, honestly though, it's not like we need the money from that aspect of your work," he says. "The movie option paid for the new house, the Greenville house sold so quickly, plus our cars are paid for."

"We still have ongoing living expenses and food and maintenance," I say, searching the night sky for answers.

"Yeah, but the interest on my 401(k) alone helps take care of most of that, not to mention all the income you're bringing in – and we're not even talking residuals yet."

I look down. He had me there.

"Trevor," I say quietly, taking his hands in mine. "It's not about the money. It's that I've finally found a career that I love so much, one that fulfills me more than any of my corporate jobs ever did. How could you take that away from me?"

"But how could you take yourself away from your family? Especially when we don't need the money?" he asks.

"That's not fair! Why is it that when a woman wants to go after her dreams, she's told she's being too ambitious?" I ask. "Men don't have to choose."

"Well, I'm asking you to choose."

"I thought everything was going so well," I say.
"It is," he answers, looking down briefly. "I mean, I like being here for the kids."

"It's just an adjustment," I try to convince him. "Once you get more settled in and meet more people, it'll get better. Believe me, I went through it."

"It's not that – I want you."

"You have me," I implore.

"Not like before. I want more of you."

"Or else what?"

Trevor looks off into the distance, the sun long having sank beneath the horizon.

Is he telling me what I think he's telling me? Am I actually going to have to choose between my career and my family?

CHAPTER 4: STRIKING OUT AND REDISCOVERING US

I almost never thought I'd see this day. Our entire family is sitting in church together. Or rather, we're kind of jumping along to the songs that we'd normally hear pumping loud in Trevor's Acura MDX – songs from Da T.R.U.T.H. and Lecrae, Christian rappers who have shown up live and in person in this hip-hop themed megachurch full of young people in an amped up atmosphere.

God is most definitely here, I can feel Him, and sense his Holy Spirit's presence in the way that I cry and bend down. I love it when I feel the Lord so closely – I definitely need Him in this moment, when I'm so confused as to what to do to make the work situation and Trevor and myself happy all at once.

"Thank You, Lord," Trevor whispers next to me, his head hung low and hands raised during an instrumental musical part of the worship as the music shifts.

Wow.

That's been the refrain for most of this day, when Trevor first surprised me by even encouraging us to attend this amazingly powerful place of worship in the first place. It's not like any staid and stuffy locale you've ever seen before – but there's an actual smoke machine that distributes a hazy cloud as the young singers play instruments and sing, interspersed with the famous rappers when it's their turn.

Talk about hyped.

There's no way Sean and Kayla are sleeping through this, nor are they slumped in their seats or laying all on my lap and complaining and asking "Can we go?" or "Is it over yet?" like the days of yore when I used to bribe them to come to church with me as Trevor stayed home.

I can literally see Trevor changing before my eyes – this selfsame man who I begged and pleaded with to come with me to church for years and join, until I gave up on the thought and delved wholeheartedly into my career and tossing hopeful prayers heavenward in Jesus' name for God to save Trevor and baptize him full of the Holy Spirit, leaving no room for evil stuff.

"There's a couple here tonight," says Pastor Tony as he holds a microphone to his mouth, raises one hand and speaks at a normal, yet emphatic level.

"God says there's a family here tonight," he continues, an unassuming man in a genuine appeal to the congregation. He pauses, as if hearing from another realm.

"Yes, there's a father and husband here tonight," Pastor Tony smiles, eyes closed. "You did the right thing man, you did the right thing by coming here."

I stare at the sandals on my feet, and catch a glimpse of something small falling onto Trevor's peanut butter colored leather shoes. I take a deep breath and begin to pray in tongues in whispers as I realize they are tears dropping from Trevor's eyes onto his shoes, with one drop staining it a bit as it rolls onto the floor.

'Not by might nor by power, but by my Spirit,' the Almighty reminds me.

"Forget what your old pastor did," Pastor Tony gets louder, "forget what your old church did. Forget the decisions your old man made…"

I can hear my husband verbalize his cry with a small wail, quite a feat from a man I've only seen shed a tear perhaps once, after his aunt died unexpectedly. I remain quiet and sway. Trevor grabs my right hand.

"You follow Christ for yourself!" Pastor Tony is now speaking loudly, but not shouting in a hateful way, more like someone would yell to encourage a team of basketball players, or warn someone about to walk into a burning building, or stepping blindly on an uncovered manhole.

"Show your family the right way to go," Pastor Tony continues. "Lean on God to be the man they need you to be. Lead your wife and children home."

With that, I feel a slight pull on my hand. Trevor has taken Sean by the hand, and I naturally grab for Kayla as the four of us walk toward the front of the large room, colorful lights rotating around us as we reach the front and join others who've done the same thing.

"Yes, yes!" Pastor Tony says, worshipping God, who has drawn a good-sized group of people to the front.

Our family kneels near the steps as a woman prays with us.

"Lord God, direct our hearts, and thank You for sending Your Son Jesus the Christ to die on the cross for us, giving us eternal life," she says.

We repeat after her, speaking through intelligible tears.

When done, I reach out before she can leave.

"Would you pray with us for an answer to our dilemma about my job?" I ask.

She smiles, but before she can speak, Trevor interjects.

"It's okay, honey," he says, accepting a tissue. "I don't want you to quit something I know you love. I'll adjust."

"Thank You, God," I breathe skyward, hugging my husband and then our kids in one big group hug.

Looking around the immense venue, with the

musicians and celebrity rappers and attendees and smoke machine and lights, I can't help but be overwhelmed with joy at the new church that my husband actually wants to attend as a family.

Beyond the significant spiritual events of the evening, a pervasive thought about work creeps in.

I wonder if they would let us film a scene or two in this place?

§ § § § § §

I am on an electric high as I near the studios, but am taken aback when I see a large group of people milling about outside the building, looking at their phones or each other.

Apollos makes a beeline for me as I walk towards our group, and our other show writers gather excitedly around me.

"What's going on?" I ask them. "Why aren't we in the building?"

"Writer's strike," Peter says quickly and succinctly, in that curt New York accent of his.

"You've gotta be kidding," I say, in disbelief. "Why are we striking? We just got started!"

Octavia shakes her head, "It's not just us. It's a WGA strike."

I'm dazed. "Another one?"

"Yep," Apollos says, looking down at a Wikipedia page on his iPad. "The last one lasted almost four months."

"I marched in that one," Octavia said. "That was in 2007 and 2008 – man, we were hurtin'."

"You should've seen the strike in '88," Peter chimes in. "That was almost six months long."

"We can't wait that long," I say. "We were just getting into the rhythm of the new shows."

Apollos looks at me intently. "We've got to!"

"But what are we demanding this time?" I ask, finally glad that I have that once elusive Writers Guild of America card in my wallet that I've wanted for years – a card that I feel gives me the right to say "we" instead of using a more distant-sounding pronoun.

"We want them to finally lock down a better deal on new media and streaming online programming," Octavia says resolutely.

"We have to stand with them," Apollos says.

"I know," I exhale. "Okay, I'm in. Where should we go now?"

"To the rallies!" he yells, like a clarion call.

"To the rallies!" Octavia repeats, smiling, just as

loudly.

"I guess we're going to the rallies," I say to Peter.

§ § § § § §

Downtown Los Angeles, we stand around listening to various big wigs speaking about writers' rights, and we cheer along at the appropriate times.

"I never knew how much exercise these things could be," I say to Apollos, as I hoist a large picket sign reading "Writers Guild of America on Strike" up high in the air.

"Here, let me take that for you," he says, making a big show of holding two huge signs with wooden handles in each hand, lifting them up and down as if he's thrusting dumbbell weights in the air.

As his biceps and deltoids show prominently, straining against the stretchy fabric of his tight muscle T-shirt, I look away.

"We don't have to stay here all day, you know," Apollos says.

"I'm hungry," Octavia says, letting the handle of her sign hit the ground as she drops it.

"Hey, we have been burning calories all day from standing and holding up signs," I say.

"Let's disappear then," he tells me.

I give Octavia a look, one that lets my eyes move from her to him quickly. I've already shared my previous emotional dilemma with her, and she knows that I'm viewing her like a new California accountability partner.

"I'll drive!" she says quickly.

"Thank you," I mouth.

§ § § § § §

"We need to show you all of L.A.," Apollos says as he sits across the table from me.

"That would be fun," I say, picking at the strawberries atop my salad, swimming in a little raspberry vinaigrette dressing.

"Aren't you hungry?" he asks me.

"Yes, but I tend to pick at my food when I'm around other people," I whisper. "I was hoping you didn't notice."

"That's what keeps you so skinny," he smiles.

"Hey guys," Octavia says, wiping pizza sauce from her mouth with a napkin. "Let's take a drive up to Mulholland Scenic Parkway."

"I'm game," I answer, pushing my salad plate away from me.

By the time the three of us snake our way up to the overlook point and park near the edge in the crowded parking lot and get out, I am in awe – and slightly afraid – of the huge height the view provides.

"This is amazing," I say, taking a panoramic photo with my iPhone 5.

"Told ya," Octavia says.

I stand up even higher on a concrete bench so that I can see even more of the surrounding vista, but I become acutely aware that my hips and waist and torso and chest are in a closer proximity to Apollos, who moves instinctively closer, holding out his hands to help me down.

His arms and whole body, from what he's told me, are tattoo free. Apollos may be younger, but he hasn't gone along with the whole "tatted up" crowd. He is attractive and clearly wanting – perhaps playing games with me, perhaps not articulating the boredom or pain he may feel being married to the wife he's chosen, or perhaps not even realizing the way the enemy is trying to use him to commit evil.

At that moment it all becomes clear to me – the chaperone that Octavia has become, the same patterns, the same look in this man's eyes below me. I've seen it before, and I've lived it before, and I know so much better.

God and I have spent so much time together, walking

in the woods through the snow and rain and sleet and great weather for me to not see the same mistake trying to reemerge it's ugly head once more.

The casting out of the lust demon by the blood of Christ that has tried to rule parts of my life is an important thing. And whether it tempted me through generational curses, or because of the promiscuity I allowed into my life whilst searching for the "Daddy love" I felt I was missing growing up, the important thing is to recognize certain predilections within ourselves and let them be broken, severed completely.

Along those lines, today I'm remembering the time when I called Pastor Smokie Norful "fine" and was corrected by a Christian sister friend I'd just met who worked in the mall during a long conversation we had.

"What were you guys talking about so long?" Trevor asked me that day as he waited around, mulling about with his oldest sister, who loves to shop.

In that way that divine connections and appointed meetings occur in our lives, I was meant to meet that black woman, who very gently corrected me and showed me myself. Sure, Pastor Norful is an attractive and talented man – but there was no reason for me to call him "fine" like that. I know he's married and I didn't even lust after him in that manner, I guess I was merely acting out of what I thought I was supposed to do.

But there's a way that as women, we can recognize and appreciate a good-looking man without it leading to a salacious place.

After that conversation with the woman in the mall, I shifted my viewpoint a bit, but it would take God using my bad encounter with Desmond to teach me and shift me to a better paradigm from the inside, a long-lasting new vista.

"So next we've got the La Brea Tar Pits, then the Griffith Observatory hike," Apollos says, pausing, grinning up at me.

Standing up so high, overlooking the lands of Los Angeles, with a gorgeous mysterious brown luxury home with a swooping roof looming overhead, I feel like a person being offered all the kingdoms of the world, if only I'd bow down to evil.

What am I doing here?

I'm not even necessarily working – although this will probably show up as a plot point in one of our coming Emmy-winning, record-shattering episodes of *Church People* – and I'm not even standing with the striking WGA workers.

I'm just playing around, running around town with a man who needs to be at home with his family. And I need to do the same.

"I'm going home to be with my husband and children," I tell Apollos, as he suddenly looks befuddled.

"Octavia, can you give me a ride back to my car?" I ask, jumping down.

"Absolutely," she says.

§ § § § § §

Trevor and I check into the Villagio Inn and Spa, and promptly fall on the fluffy bed.

"I wonder if this is the same exact room we had before," I say, staring close into his pretty brown eyes.

Trevor looks around, from the logs next to the fireplace, to the TV and beyond the sliding glass door patio.

"You know, it could be," he says.

Later, we are lying around in the afterglow of love, each of us with our tablets in hand, taking sips of champagne from our respective flutes.

"Look at this," I say, tilting my iPad screen toward him as I swipe past photos of us in various locales.
"Oh wow," he laughs, "look how young Sean looks, trying to flex his muscles."

We crack up at the photo of our son from 2010, looking like such a little boy.

"Houston...Chicago...New York," I say, continually scrolling. "We've been so many great places and have taken so many great vacations."

"And I'm glad Mommy and Daddy flew in to watch Kayla and Sean so we could take this one alone!" Trevor says, raising his glass in the air near me.

I grab for my glass and gently click his. "Here, here!"

"To us," he says.

"Amen," I confirm.

After a few more scrolls back through the Facebook photos that load more images backwards, from 2013 to 2012 to 2011 to 2010, I land on a pic of Desmond and our tech team back at church in the control room, a few of us smiling in our all-black gear.

Desmond stands in the front next to a 21-year-old team member, his hand resting on her arm as they smile. I am in the back as usual, being the tall one, as Sherrie smiles on my left-hand side and other various members of the team smile and pose.

Trevor looks away from the photo almost at the same time I tilt my iPad away from his uncomfortable gaze. Neither one of us necessarily likes focusing on that part of our lives – and I train myself not even to look in Desmond's eyes in the photo, because I don't want to look at him ever again in life.

For at least one of the group photos that I appeared in with Desmond I went through and untagged myself. But that one I left alone, for now, not wanting to do anything wrong that would call attention to the fact that I was viewing the photo. Perhaps I will un-tag my name some day.

The other photos from Christmastime with Desmond's wife, however, as Sherrie took pictures of us and another woman playing around and posing like *Charlie's Angels*, such as women tend to do, I left those alone.

First of all, it probably was a matter of vanity, because I like the way I look in those pics, all nice and skinny with my collarbones showing prominently above my décolletage. Only four months after meeting Desmond, I'd already begun to lose weight and look better, for him and myself and the other guys I was hanging around.

But I know a deeper part of me left those tags of my name on those photos simply to remember Desmond's wife, to think of my role in any of the pain I caused her just by growing too close to her husband.

I realize now I could've been a much better friend to her by being on her side more, like I did the night I agreed it wasn't a good idea for him to watch a boxing match all late at night with that 21-year-old in his home.

Yeah, I'm sure my own wayward jealousy was a part of that, but as a wife myself, I also empathized with her feelings on the matter. If I would have stayed in that vein, and made a point to befriend and speak with her a lot more about the happenings on the team instead of allowing Desmond and I to grow so close together, things would've been different.

However, I liked her at first, but a part of me grew not

to like her, similar to the way I've felt about other women – especially ones who tend to ramble on and on incessantly in conversations without taking much of a break to listen to the other person and figure out what's going on in their life.

But that's no excuse to "catch feelings" for a married man, or vice versa. So part of me leaves those photos of us up on Facebook just to remind myself of how I never want to act again. It could've been very easy for me to curtail certain conversations – or never to have touched Desmond's thigh to begin with – something I told myself I'd tell no one, but ended up writing it, because the truth does indeed set us free.

"Yep, when your husband call me today and we talked about such-and-such," I could've told her, letting her know how much we were talking during the day.

But then again, God used my writing to eventually tell her everything she needed to know. And so the pics are a reminder to me of a period I never want to live through again, and a manner that I never want to act in again.

"Do you want to watch *Temptation*?" Trevor asks, having figured out how to scroll through the list of available movies to watch.

"Yes, *mos def*," I answer, glad to watch the movie once more, thinking of how my husband and I double dated with another couple back in Greenville when we saw it the first time.

"I can't remember if I liked it the first time," Trevor

says.

"I think you were concentrating on why one woman was on the phone in the theater, and all those girls behind us were talking," I say.

"Oh yeah," Trevor laughs. "Maybe I'll hear it all this time."

As he orders the movie, I think of how, when the four of us went out to dinner at *The Olive Garden* back east after the movie, the waiter mistakenly asked me if I was with my friend's husband.

"Not after that movie we just saw," I said, and the four of us chuckled, fresh off the sad high of the cautionary tale about a young wife who cheats on her husband with a slick and rich entrepreneur named Harley, a guy who nearly completely ruins her life.

Sometimes I think of Desmond and wonder what happened, like the unanswered ending for Harley in the movie. I think of Desmond in some way every day – maybe just a passing thought here and there some days, or more pensively on others. I've learned not to fight it, like when I would try not to think of him anymore. I realize it's like telling myself not to think of a purple elephant.

All you'll see is purple elephants.

"I wish him the best," I used to tell Sherrie, and she'd get mad that I was being so forgiving in the face of his lies.

My Grief Recovery letter that I read to her about him revealed a bit more of my intensive feelings, but I never got too out of pocket, because I kept remembering what Jesus said about how to treat those we're mad at or feel bad feelings about:

But I say unto you, Love your enemies, bless them that curse you, do good to them that hate you, and pray for them who despitefully use you, and persecute you.

Because of that, I don't wish much ill will on Desmond, despite whatever lies he tried to spread about me, because he is still my brother in Christ – and what kind of person who claims to be a bondservant of Christ would want to see a family destroyed?

Maybe only part of me understands why Desmond reacted the foul way he did after his wife or whatever suck-up church person found my writings online and then snitched to the pastor.

But I told the truth about the situation. Sure, I fictionalized some scenes, but I didn't lie on him and the truth does indeed set me free. Perhaps that's why God let me stay in Greenville and not get removed like Desmond and his wife, and eventually the pastor – at least from over that church.

The parts of the screenplay that I consolidated and changed were me touching his thigh – I only moved that from the control room to Desmond's home, but I told the truth about him taking my picture and telling me I had "subtle curves" and us giggling and him telling both me and the 21-year-old that "I need you both to F me," when he was trying to find a cute and clever way to say forgive him.

I don't know if he really stared after the young lady's butt when she walked across the room, because I was too busy looking at her butt myself, seeing as though she was wearing sweatpants with writing on the behind – so that part may have been untrue, though Sherrie recalls him looking.

Heck, Desmond should've been kissing my feet thinking about the secrets that I didn't include in writing, and still won't, even though he lied about me, causing one deacon to nearly cry when he discovered Desmond was still texting me while telling folks at church that I was the one who chased him.

I guess he felt like he had to "save face" and "protect his family," like Pastor Jameson said Desmond was doing, after the pastor kicked me off the tech team.

Like hell. All they were trying to do was suppress the truth and make themselves look good with a bunch of lies and half-truths and cover-ups.

The other part of the screenplay that was fictionalized was when Desmond said "I need this in my life" while in my living room, he was looking at the PlayStation Eye, not directly at me, like I made it seem in the script when I wrote that his character was coveting another man's wife.

But plenty of other actions showed he had done just that with me.

"You made me look like a womanizer," he cried on the phone with me the last time I talked to him.

Yeah, no kidding. Aren't you the same man who had to have a meeting about the comment you made to the 21-year-old woman on the team, and then got too close to me emotionally?

"We could've been in this thing for five years," Desmond had told me, a married woman.

And thusly, I've said inappropriate things to him as well. The difference was that I owned up to my wrongdoings (wrong dongs, all right, like I just mistakenly typed) and let myself disappear from that church location, while he got to remain and tried to yuck it up with more girls and pretend that Seine just "flipped out" out of nowhere.

Desmond was on the deacon track, and thought he had things all sewed up in the bag, with his pastor buddy he manipulated right by his side. But then Desmond and family ended up going back to his hometown – an odd place to return to, unless that was part of the plan all along. I don't know if it was, but I'll bet if he'd gotten a real successful job back home, he would've probably already let everyone know about it.

I wonder if they had to move in with his mom, or got their own home. Either way, none of this matters, and that's when I think to myself, "God speed!"

As for Pastor Jameson, his story is still being written.

After the church split caused a lot of pain and confusion, the jury is still out on how that will end. I used to go to noon Bible study down at the main branch of church, and I'd see him still sometimes.

One time I wrote and prayed about God haunting folks in a good way, waking them up at 3 a.m. and such and people doing right by me, and the next day, Pastor Jameson preached and talked about being up at 3 a.m. on his laptop because he couldn't sleep.

I kind of smiled to myself.

When things like that came true, along with other things I'd written about in the script, like me falling on my bike and hurting my leg a little, a wound that bled, and it happened in real life – though thankfully I didn't fall as hard in real life as I'd written about – it showed me the power of my writing.

I've learned to write happy endings, if God's going to help me use this holy imagination for wonderful things.

Another part of the screenplay that came true was when I was asked back to the ministry after a period of time. It perhaps took longer in real life for Sherrie and an elder to ask me to come back, longer than the less than 90 days I'd written about, but it felt good all the same.

It's interesting that in my script I wrote about not really giving them an answer on it, but in real life, I felt a big old "no" on that one. After all, I'm not about the church games and people faking and hiding their true sins and real nasty selves and trying to kiss up to pastors because they think that will give them some authority and wealth and importance.

I'm more about following the true Hollywood dreams that have been in my heart for so long – but now using them in a way that can glorify God's goodness and lead people to the power and healing of Christ Jesus.

Last night when I was Googling around and putting my maiden name in double quotes so I could find anything written about my full name, I found a reference to a screenplay I'd copyrighted way back in 1996, and that showed me that I've been after this dream for nearly 20 years.

I'm so grateful that it's finally come my way, right in the Lord's perfect way and timing so that I'm mature enough to receive it and not throw it away.

"Beloved, I pray that above all else you prosper and be in good health, even as your soul prospers," the Apostle John prayed, and that's a Scripture that resonates with me now.

It may have taken me 44 years to get the message about trying to live better and in a way that hopefully pleases God more, but at least I'm here now while I'm still young enough to enjoy it all, and my family can benefit from it, too, unlike those who are 88 and finally get the message.

Now I can share that message with others in an honest and balanced way that doesn't try to whitewash my own actions, or leave too much stuff hidden, all the while lying about trying to "protect the church's integrity" or some such other nonsense people say when they are really covering up their own dirty deeds that are in full view of God.

I'd much rather see compassion shown to a sinner or saint, than some Holly Roller pretending like they've got it all together – just because they don't smoke or whatever – and look down their holy noses at everybody else. That's the attitude that's primed for a fall, big time, if they don't "humble yourself under the mighty hand of God so that in due time He will exalt you."

And I'm feeling exalted by God right now, due to his grace and favor. I feel like a positive resurgence like Da T.R.U.T.H., whose album "The Whole Truth" experienced a lot more success than the "Fresh" songs of his former mentor, Tye Tribbett.

There was a big scandal in the church world when it was rumored that Tribbett slept with a woman outside of his marriage, so Tribbett's wife turned to Da T.R.U.T.H. for comfort, and ending up sleeping with him, a married man.

Desmond and I used to recite so many lines about adultery from "The Whole Truth" album to each other, probably because we could sense ourselves growing so close to that type of situation. But what I love about it is that Da T.R.U.T.H. put much more of his honest self and literal truth into his lyrics – forget that "airing your dirty laundry" line us black people pull out too much to try and cover our own butts – and the success of his sales show that fact.

Heck, I only learned about the album when Trevor downloaded it, probably after he saw it hit #1 on iTunes – not just as the top Christian rap album, but top rap album – and I later downloaded it as well. I was going to burn Desmond a CD from it, but he already had it.

Tye Tribbett kind of danced around the situation, and his "Fresh" song is good, but Da T.R.U.T.H.'s is in much heavier rotation in my iTunes library. So honesty pays. Literally.

But Desmond chose the lying route, and I believe he paid for that in his own way. Literally. After all, how stupid could some people be to see Desmond and I together so much at church, to watch him smiling at me and us chatting excitedly and hugging one another and spending so much time alone talking, as if the world around us had melted away – and then turn around and believe his lies that I chased after him?

Seriously?

It was a dark time at the end of 2011, but God's mighty hand upheld me and sustained me, and before too long the favor began to swing around in my direction, without me having to lie or scheme or blast certain folks in the process.

I learned to benefit from the sweet fellowship of being with Rabboni each morning, and I never want to give up my time with the Lord.

§ § § § § §

I cry watching Tyler Perry's *Temptation: Confessions of a Marriage Counselor* movie once more. Trevor has almost fallen asleep under my hands, as I instinctively rub the hairs on his head in circles, using firm strokes.

It's the scene where the main character Judith is a mess, having been beat up by her boyfriend Harley, the rich guy who tempted her and drew her away from her "good guy" husband who has come to rescue her.

After her husband lifts her out of the bathtub, she says, "We can fix it, right?"

Her cuckolded husband is so hurt – they grew up together, and now their marriage was ending. It is something about that scene, and the previous one that shows Judith breaking up with her husband, and telling him that she and Harley could pay for counseling to help her man get over the divorce, that makes a tear stream out of my eye – unlike when we watched the movie in the theaters when it first came out.

Suddenly, Trevor's Galaxy starts vibrating with an urgent sound. He startles and answers it, sitting up.

"What? Right now?" he asks into the phone. "We'll be right there."

"What is it?" I ask.

"Mommy had to call 911 for Daddy," he says. "We

need to go home."

CHAPTER 5: A WONDERFUL CHANGE HAS COME

Turns out it was a false alarm and Trevor's dad is just fine. It was a bit of a gas attack and perhaps he hit the panic button, but it turns out it was the perfect opportunity for him to face his own mortality.

After all, it was Mr. Paulsen and I who had got into that argument back in Greenville years ago when Trevor was in the hospital due to his enlarged heart, and I had visions of him not making it for split seconds – but God healed him perfectly.

When Trevor was still in the ICU and being moved to another room, I saw one man tell someone on his phone that "John died" and I saw him hug a person as they got off the elevator.

By the grace of God alone, that grieving person experiencing loss wasn't Mr. Paulsen or me, and we'd escaped death once more this time with him being okay. But during those days, I'd pulled out the cross with John 3:16 written on it, and asked Sean's granddad to listen to his grandson reading the pivotal verse.

"I've read the Bible," he said, somewhat snippily, finally getting down to the fact that he said he felt he needed to feel the whole Christian heaven/hell thing inside his own heart.

All these years later, it seems he's feeling it – and his fear of hospitals was a fear of uncertainty over where he was going after he died, like I told him. He's a lot calmer now, and isn't so reticent about Jesus things anymore.

Mr. Paulsen and our whole family visit the hip-hop church and they turn their lives over to Jesus for real one night – not only Trevor's dad, but his mom and sisters and brothers-in-law and all of our kids and we ourselves recommit to putting God first in our lives.

We've ended up in this manor – or the Paulsen Compound, if you will – that we've always talked about creating. Here we have Trevor's parents and our family members and friends living close by -- or at least having a cool vacation spot when they want to get out of Greenville and Chicago and escape the harsh cold winters.

We've been taking trips to national parks, skiing with the family and friends, visiting Lake Tahoe, and many other places I've always wanted to see, free from the pallor of gray skies back east.

I was hesitant about leaving some of my friends in Greenville, like Sherrie and her daughter, who had become good friends with my daughter. And there was also another good friend Grace and her husband, who I had met through church years ago.

It is taken years to build some of these friendships including another friend Michelle and her husband, not to mention the friends that Trevor made through his job, however sometimes change can be really good.

And I realized I didn't need to shy away from moving to California, because I was fearing the time it would take to build new friendships, thinking they would take another nine years or seven years or so.

This dilemma reminded me of those lyrics from the Culture Club group from the 1980s when lead singer Boy George said that time makes lovers feel like they have something real, but you and me we know they got nothing but time.

So I realize that I didn't need to hold on to friendships just because I had a bunch of time invested in them, and especially not if it were time to grow or at least allow the changing breeze to shift us – and collect the best memories from them, and if they were meant to last God would keep them as my divine connections.

Because after all imagine the new divine connections that were waiting for us in California that by the grace of God we didn't miss.

It's like I'm looking back on the more private trail

where we used to walk – God and I – during those days in Greenville, when I walked and prayed in tongues for the Desmond and Pastor Jameson situation to change, and little did I know He would improve my life so mightily after that time.

The Lord has taught me how to be platonic friends with men – and after the writers strike ended and I went back to work, with decent hours, he showed me how to relate to coworkers, both males and females, the proper way, without sticking my neck out too far for some Casanova where it didn't belong.

It's better that way anyway. I'm always that girl that the guys want, but respect because I won't go there with them.

God has shown me the "season, reason or lifetime person," those people who were just meant to be in my life for a short or long season of time, compared to those who simply came into my life for a reason – like Desmond and his wife, to teach me how I never want to act again – and those lifetime folks, like my Trevor, who is growing more in the Lord and amazing me every day.

Beyond that, Sherrie's marriage has been restored, and after her cupcake business took off and she relocated out west near us, it's like looking at a whole new family when we view them.

Even more exciting is watching Trevor changing for the better, and developing new skills and a career that he loves, even as the children are making more real friends and growing to love their schools and activities as well even more – looking forward to driving and the teenage years and everything.

§ § § § § §

"What do you think about this?" Trevor says happily one day as I come home, and he's got paperwork spread across the table in the back patio, along with the kids as they do their homework.

"What is it?" I ask, kissing them all, sitting down next to him.

"It's a charity called 'Send Money' that we can use to help people who just flat out need money," he explains. "They will just contact the email address and write us their story, and the amount of money they need."

"But how will we know who's legit and who's lying?" I ask.

"God will tell us," Trevor says, and my heart does a little leap. "We can trust Him to lead us to the emails that are true and whether we need to answer it and send a single mother $500, let's say, so her power won't get shut off."

"I love it!" I nearly scream.

"Like Jesus did, it would be a way for us to help people in need in a practical way, and also let them know God loves them and heard their prayers."

My eyes well up with tears, and excitement grows in the depth of my belly.

"So let's figure out what we need to do to set it up."

Trevor shows me a paper, "I'm already ahead of you. I've got the financial accounting information and the PayPal account and everything. You want to take a walk?"

"Yes, Lord!" I answer.

Trevor and I have been taking walks around our neighborhood, the same affluent black neighborhood where Johnny Cochran once lived that I once saw on a 20/20 report and never forgot, where our new family "compound" exists.

These strolls together have been the best times to connect and strategize and find out all sorts of things about each other – and a great method of planning our next steps.

It's out of those walks that our charity was born, plus I was able to learn of a perfect role that Trevor actually wanted to take on at the studio – the kind of person that's invaluable to a show by catching any inconsistencies in the things the characters say or do, and helps the continuity by figuring out if a person was wearing something one way in once scene, and then a collar flips up or something else noticeable happens in the editing process that viewers might catch.

Trevor's always been good at that kind of stuff.

§ § § § § §

Our family and friends are all in our living room as we exit our bedroom, dressed to the nines.

"Oooohhh," says Trevor's father. "Beyoncé and Kanye."

"You mean Beyoncé and Jay-Z," Trevor says.

"Whatever, y'all look good!" Trevor's mom says.

We feel good, finally on the way to those award ceremonies to walk the red carpet and sit and chat with superstars and sip the bubbly while waiting for our names to be called as we have a great time with the writing staff – not just of the acclaimed TV series, but the matching feature film that did big box office numbers and garnered its own share of praise as well.

When the moment happens and the Golden Globe is in my hand, and I'm on stage, I'm overwhelmed with a sense of joy and acceptance – not only from my peers and viewers, which is quite nice, but also from a much deeper place beyond the third heaven that really counts.

My life is full. I've got the job and husband and children and family and friends I love, and my work in the world is meaningful. Just like Trevor said, our charity is helping lots of people not only get out of financial binds, but is letting them know God loves them and is saving folks by the multitude by helping them see the

Christ who is there all along, even as you read this.

It's telling that only after we talked that night about setting up the charity, and not hoarding monies for ourselves just to buy multiple mansions and fancy clothes, but to use it for a higher purpose and calling, did our TV show and movie and careers take off – as if God was pouring so much wisdom and funding into the venture.

We've been privileged to read a lot of incredible stories, and in turn, Trevor and I have been able to share all the ways God has bonded our marriage and family together via his love, despite all of our mistakes.

The show is turning into a long-running series that the Lord can use to fund our retirements many times over, no matter when it ends. Whenever that is, I want to ride this train until I ride it all the way to heaven, just like a chariot of fire.

We are right where we are supposed to be, doing what we were put on this planet to do, and I'm loving the journey, in Jesus' name. Amen.